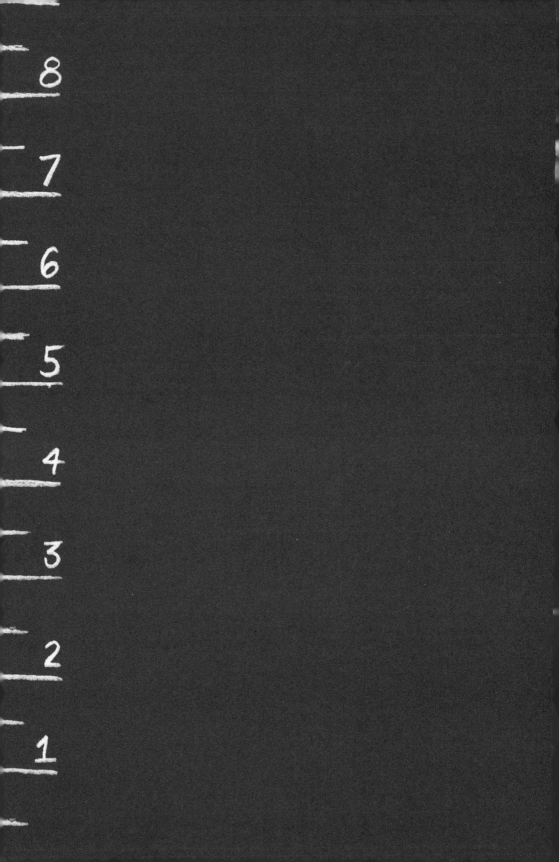

peg + cat
THE PIRATE PROBLEM

A LEVEL 2 READER

JENNIFER OXLEY
+ BILLY ARONSON

CANDLEWICK
ENTERTAINMENT

This book is based on the TV series *Peg + Cat*.
Peg + Cat is produced by The Fred Rogers Company.
Created by Jennifer Oxley and Billy Aronson.
The Pirate Problem is based on a television script by
Billy Aronson and background art by Amy DeLay.
Art assets assembled by Alex Kudeyar.
The PBS KIDS logo is a registered mark of the Public
Broadcasting Service and is used with permission.

pbskids.org/peg

First edition 2017

Library of Congress Catalog Card Number pending
ISBN 978-0-7636-9786-0 (hardcover)
ISBN 978-0-7636-9789-1 (paperback)

17 18 19 20 21 22 APS 10 9 8 7 6 5 4 3 2 1

Printed in Humen, Dongguan, China

This book was typeset in OPTITypewriter.
The illustrations were created digitally.

Candlewick Entertainment
an imprint of Candlewick Press
99 Dover Street
Somerville, Massachusetts 02144

visit us at www.candlewick.com

Contents

Chapter 1
THE SANDWICH

Peg and Cat were on an island.
They were ready to eat their
favorite sandwich--cheese and
pickles!

"Uh-oh," said Cat. "We only
brought one sandwich!"

"And there are two of us,"
said Peg.

Peg and Cat had a big
problem. They were both hungry!

"You take the sandwich,"
said Peg.

"No, you," said Cat.

"Me?" said Peg.

"Unless you think I should," said Cat.

Cat took the sandwich. It tore into two pieces.

"You amazing Cat!" said Peg.
"You turned one big sandwich
into two small sandwiches. Now
there is one for each of us."

Chapter 2
THE PIRATES

"Arr! Arr! Arr!"

Peg and Cat heard noises.

Pirates jumped out from behind a tree.

"We smell pickle juice," said a Pirate.

"Yummy!" said another Pirate.

"Sorry, Pirates. We ate the sandwiches," said Peg.

"But we are hungry. When Pirates get hungry, we get cranky. And when we get cranky, we sing really badly," said the Pirates.

"We don't want you to get cranky," said Peg.

"We don't have any food to give you," said Cat.

"Then you've got a REALLY BIG PROBLEM!" said the Pirates.

Chapter 3

PIRATE FOOD

Cat went to look for some Pirate food.

He bumped into a tree. A mango fell down. Ow!

"Do Pirates like mangoes?" asked Peg.

"Yucky! Icky! Yuck!" said
the Pirates.

"How about papayas?" said Peg.

"Yucko! Ick!"

"Pirates are very picky
eaters," said the Pirates.

Peg saw a banana tree.

"Check out that big banana," said Peg.

"That must be the Great Banana!" said a Pirate.

Cat shook the tree. But the banana did not come down.

"Silly Cat. The Great Banana will not come down until it's ready," said a Pirate.

"Do you like peaches?" asked
Peg.

"Pirates love peaches!"

The Pirates ran to a peach
tree and shook it.

Peaches fell down on
everyone!

Peg counted the peaches.

One, two, three, four,
five, six, seven, eight, nine,
ten, eleven, twelve, thirteen,
fourteen, fifteen, sixteen
peaches!

The Pirates started
fighting.

"These peaches are mine!"

"You got more than me!"

"Stop!" said Peg. "There are
enough peaches for all of you."

Chapter 4
FAIR SHARING

Peg and Cat's friend Ramone
walked by.

Peg said, "Can you help
us, Ramone? These Pirates are
getting cranky. They are really
hungry. They totally love
peaches. But they don't know
how to divide them up."

"Have you Pirates ever tried fair sharing?" asked Ramone.

"What is fair sharing?" asked a Pirate.

"Fair sharing means dividing things up evenly," said Ramone. "Like when I play cards with my friends. Everyone gets the same number of cards."

Cat handed out cards. Everyone got the same number.

"Just like that, but with peaches," said Ramone.

The Pirates didn't understand.

"We play cards with the peaches?" asked a Pirate.

"We eat the cards?" asked another Pirate.

"No. You can divide up
these peaches just like you
would divide up cards," said
Ramone.

"We'll show you how,"
said Peg.

She handed out the peaches.

Ramone sang:

"One for you and you and
you and you.
And one more for you and
you and you."

"And me, too!" sang a Pirate.

Everyone joined in:
"One, two, three, four.
Nobody got less. Nobody got more.
Four peaches each right there.
Everybody got their fair share!"

Chapter 5
THE PEACH THIEF

Ramone left.

"Now you Pirates all have the same number of peaches," said Peg. "You can finally eat and not be cranky!"

A monkey watched from the peach tree.

"I only have two peaches!
Did you swipe me peaches?"
asked a Pirate.

"Never!"

"I only have one peach,"
said another Pirate.

"Peach thief!"

"Don't fight. They're only
peaches," said Peg.

Cat held up his paws.
The Pirates stopped fighting.

"Look! That
monkey in the
tree took your
peaches!"
said Cat.

"Give them back, you monkey meanie," said a Pirate.

"Cat and I can get your peaches back. We have two amazing powers," said Peg. "Cat can speak monkey."

"Ooh! Ooh! Ee! Ee!" said Cat.

"And I can do addition," said Peg.

Peg said to the first
Pirate, "You have two peaches.
You need one, two more peaches
to make four!" she counted. "Two
plus two equals four."

Peg said to another Pirate,
"You have one peach. You need
one, two, three more to make
four!"

"Ooh, ooh, ee," said Cat.
The monkey threw three
peaches down from the tree.
"One plus three equals
four!" said Peg. "One, two,
three, four! Now everybody
has four."
"Yo-ho-ho-ho!" said the
Pirates.

BOOM!

"What was that?"
asked Peg.

"The Great Banana
has landed!" said
a Pirate.

Chapter 6
PROBLEM SOLVED

"Who wants peaches when I can have the Great Banana?" asked a Pirate.

The Pirates started fighting again.

"You Pirates are never going to stop fighting and eat," said Peg.

"I am TOTALLY FREAKING OUT!" said Peg.

Cat held up his paws.

"Cat is right. I should count backward from four to calm down," said Peg. "Four, three, two, one."

Peg noticed Cat sharing cards fairly with the parrot.

"That's it, you amazing,
genius Cat!" said Peg.
She hugged Cat.

"We can divide up the Great Banana fairly. Then the Pirates will be happy!"

"Yo-ho!" said the Pirates.

"So, because we knew about sharing fairly and addition, we've kept the Pirates from singing really badly."

"Math really saved our
ears," said Cat. He gave a
piece of the Great Banana to
everyone.

Peg and Cat sang:
"Problem solved!
The problem is solved.
We solved the problem.
Problem solved!"

8
7
6
5
4
3
2
1